Haniel Long was born in 1888 in Rangoon. He lived in
various parts of the United States, finally settling in New
Mexico. He was a poet and a journalist, and at one time
organized a non-profit cooperative publishing house.
Since its first publication in 1936, *The Marvellous
Adventure of Cabeza de Vaca* has attracted an ever-growing
band of admirers. Haniel Long died in 1956.

CONDITIONS OF SALE

HANIEL LONG

The Marvellous
Adventure
of Cabeza de Vaca

also Malinche

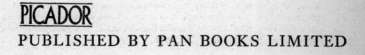
PICADOR
PUBLISHED BY PAN BOOKS LIMITED

First published in Great Britain 1972 by
Souvenir Press (Educational & Academic) Ltd
and simultaneously in Canada by
J. M. Dent & Sons (Canada) Ltd
This Picador edition published 1975 by
Pan Books Ltd, Cavaye Place, London SW10 9PG
© Haniel Long, Anton Long and Frontier Press 1939, 1969
Printed in Great Britain by
Richard Clay (The Chaucer Press) Ltd,
Bungay, Suffolk

ISBN 0 330 24383 7

To D.G.B.

Contents

Note One

Along in late November 1528, a handful of Spaniards, survivors of an ill-starred expedition to Florida, were washed ashore in the Gulf of Mexico, some think near the present site of Galveston. One of these men was Nuñez Cabeza de Vaca, thirty-eight years old, the lieutenant of the expedition, an adaptable man with some secret of growth in him. Despite the privations he had endured, this Nuñez led two other Spaniards and a Moor on a journey across the entire continent, barefoot and naked, which occupied them eight years.

After he reached Mexico City, Nuñez wrote a letter to his King, relating what had befallen him. It begins as the usual story of a European adventurer who leaves home to exploit people. But Nuñez little by little finds out that people are his brothers and sisters, and feels genuine concern for them. Stories require the right audience, and he seems afraid that His Majesty might not be interested in what he has to say, for it is the story of a disaster in

Spanish colonial history and in the King's personal finances. In the world of the individual, none the less, it is a story of triumph, however lackadaisical the manner of its telling.

My account of Nuñez is not the account he sent the King, apart of course from the actual facts. But I believe it to be the account he wished to send the King. I preserve the core of his narrative, as translated by Fanny Bandelier, and I try to show what, quite plainly, was happening to the spirit of the man. That is, I allow him to speak as though unafraid of his King and his times. I wish him to address us four hundred years later, in this world of ours where human relation is still the difficult problem, and exploitation the cancer.

Nuñez found the limitless within the narrowly limited. He helped when he had no means of helping, and gave when he had nothing to give. So, what is interesting is that at a certain point he ceases to be a historical personage and becomes a symbol. If he were alive today, he would be free to bring into the open the inwardness of his adventure. Thus he would greatly concern the present western world and our entire human world, for we are his proper audience.

In his emergency Nuñez slides out of theories and prejudices which unfit one to live on. Possibly the capacity to survive depends upon courage of spirit to accept one's fate. Possibly also, danger can be a real benefit to the physical man. Nuñez was remarkably flexible; he had what seems unlimited courage, unlimited strength. To him life itself was not different from hardship and danger, life *was* these things, and they are what make life good. His plight was hopeless, but he set in motion a train of thought and action which saved him. My attention wanders from the perfunctory narrative to the thing he refrains from confiding to the royal ear. That thing is a mystical feeling about the increase of life in a man from effort and from taking thought of his fellows. The weather-beaten explorer of the XVIth century, lost in a thorny land among copper-coloured savages and facing a blank future, discovered religion to be a reality of which he had never dreamt. His effort, his feeling for others, take novel paths; but underneath, quite apparently, lies an ageless and universal experience.

Note Two

The *Naufragios* ('Shipwrecks') of Nuñez Cabeza
de Vaca first appeared at Zamora in 1542. It was this
rare first edition which Mrs Bandelier translated as
one of the volumes of the 'Trail Makers' series (*The
Journey of Alvar Nuñez Cabeza de Vaca and His
Companions from Florida to the Pacific 1528–1536.*
Tr. Fanny Bandelier with Introduction by Ad. F.
Bandelier. New York. A. S. Barnes and Co. 1905).
In 1555 the *Naufragios*, reprinted with minor
changes, was included in the first edition of the
Comentarios a narrative in which Nuñez relates the
events of his South American expedition. This edi-
tion of the 'Shipwrecks' was translated into English
in 1851 by T. Buckingham Smith, under the title
The Narrative of Alvar Nuñez Cabeça de Vaca.
An edition of Smith's translation, with many ad-
ditions, appeared in New York in 1871, with John
Gilmary Shea as editor. This annotated edition
of *The Narrative* under the editorial supervision
of Frederick W. Hodge of the Bureau of American

Ethnology is included in the series 'Original Narratives of Early American History' (*Spanish Explorers in the Southern United States 1528–1543*. Charles Scribner's Sons. New York. 1907). Morris Bishop's *The Odyssey of Cabeza de Vaca* (Century Co. 1933) is a biographical account of Nuñez, as drawn from the 'Shipwrecks', the 'Commentaries', and other sources, such as the records of the trial which clouded the last years of the explorer.

Preface

By Henry Miller

Ever since making the journey through *The Air-conditioned Nightmare*, I have been obsessed by the thought that the greatest misfortune which ever visited the white man took place in this continent. Even as a child I was impressed by the story of how the Indians greeted the first white comers as gods. Later, as a man, and as an American particularly, the shameful record of our relations with the Indians saddened me to a degree beyond anything I had ever felt in connection with man's inhumanity to man. Still later I came to look upon this phase of our history in another way, an even sadder way, I might say. I saw the refusal of the white man to play the rôle which was expected of him as an opportunity lost, an opportunity indeed which man perhaps will never have again.

Then came the story of Cabeza de Vaca, of the miracles he accomplished not only for himself but for others. It was the first bright spot I encountered in the bloody legend created by the *conquistadores*. It is a bright spot in the history of man, I should add, for, as the author states in his preface, Nuñez ceases at a certain point to be an historical personage and becomes a symbol. It is this view of the Journey which makes me prefer his account above the others; this interlinear method lifts the drama to a plane whereupon it may be compared with other great spiritual events in the chain of man's ceaseless effort towards self-liberation. For me the importance of this historical record lies not in the fact that de Vaca and his men were the first Europeans to cross the American continent, that they blazed a trail which other explorers were to follow, or that their peregrinations proved the existence of a land mass of continental proportions north of New Spain, or even that by his flaming protests de Vaca brought to an end the barbarous slave raids in that region, but that in the midst of his ordeals, after years of fruitless, bitter wanderings, the man who was once a warrior and a conqueror should be able to say: 'I shall teach the world how to conquer by gentleness, not by slaughter.' For in the course of his tribulations – and triumphs – Cabeza de Vaca finally came to understand that 'as much as a man is before God so much is he, and no more,' to use the words of St Francis. The Journey is the simple, heart-breaking record of a man stripped of everything, and obliged to act out every moment of his life in the sight of God.

Terrible as it was to be separated from his companions, terrible as it was to be naked and hungry for days and weeks, sometimes months on end, terrible and humiliating as it was to be made a slave by the people they had come to conquer, the worst, as the Interlinear rightly emphasizes, 'lay in parting little by little with the thoughts that clothe the soul of a European, and most of all the idea that a man attains a strength through dirk and dagger . . .' How eloquent are the Spaniard's simple words when, near the end of the Journey, he meets up with other members of the expedition who had been laying waste the land and leading the Indians into slavery. 'In facing these marauders,' he writes, 'I was compelled to face the Spanish gentleman I myself had been eight years before.'

This theme recurs again and again: the man I was versus the man I now am. The conversion was not only thorough and complete but alive in his consciousness to a degree almost unbearable to read of. At this point I must again pay tribute to Haniel Long for having the courage to recreate the narrative imaginatively. 'To the understanding of such days and events this additional narrative becomes necessary, like a real figure to walk beside a ghost.' This passage occurs in the Interlinear, after it has been related how the miracles were effected by de Vaca and his companions. And then comes a colloquy between de Vaca and the one called Andrés. And Andrés says: 'It is not miracles these people need. They need everything fate stript us of in bringing us amongst them naked and on equal terms.' To which de Vaca replies: 'Let the truth be said, Andrés: "All that we learned across the water we have had to throw away. Only what we learned in our mothers' arms has stayed with us to help others." '

There has been a tendency on the part of commentators, when referring to these miracles, to adopt an ambiguous attitude. Unable to deny the truth of the occurrences, they seek to explain them away by insinuating that consciously or otherwise the Spaniards did not imitate the Indian Shamans. They commend the modesty of the Spaniards in attributing their success to the direct aid of divine power, but in the same breath they attempt to excuse the exaggerations and misconceptions born of an inflamed imagination. By this attitude they seem to me to evade the question of miracles altogether, for if the powers of de Vaca and his men are thus rendered suspect, what of the powers of the

Shamans? This question of power was one which greatly concerned the Spaniards. 'What occupied me,' reads the narrative, 'was whether I could master, whether indeed it was for me to master – perhaps being a self-directing power that came through me.' 'Being Europeans,' we read again, 'we thought we had given away to doctors and priests our ability to heal . . . *We were more than we thought we were*.' This is repeated, 'To be more than I thought I was – a sensation utterly new to me.' They speak of their self-consciousness in perform-ing the cures before one another. And then occurs this significant statement: 'Alone in this wilderness no tissue of the body hindered the mysterious power.'

I am aware, of course, that much of this is 'interlinear', how much I do not care. The im-portant thing to bear in mind is precisely what the Interlinear brings out, namely, that the civilized European of four centuries ago had lost something which the Indians still possessed. None of our medicine men, despite their superior knowledge and equipment, are capable of performing these miracu-lous cures. That the Spaniards acquired their healing powers only when their own lives were threatened seems to have been overlooked. Had they been shrewd and cunning, observant of the practices of the Shamans, they would have exploited these powers long before they had reached such an extremity. Nothing is explained by attributing their partial or probable success to 'a new and striking procedure'. What we are interested in knowing is – how and why did these methods work, and, if they worked, why not now?

Perhaps the answer to this conundrum is best given by de Vaca himself at the close of the narrative. 'The power of maintaining life in others lives within each of us, and from each of us does it recede when unused.' This answer will always remain a challenge to those who, putting their hope and trust in external government, deny all individual responsibility. Never was there a time when this delusion held more sway than today. The whole trend of the times is towards surrender of individual power and authority. In spite of this, miracles have been accomplished, but of what order and at what price! Only time will tell whether, as de Vaca says, 'our communal life dries up our milk.'

I believe, and that is why I shall never cease to talk about this little book, that the experience of this lone, forsaken Spaniard in the wilderness of America puts to nought the whole democratic experiment of modern times. I believe that if he were to come alive today, and be shown the wonders and the horrors of our time, he would revert instantly to the simple, efficacious way of life he chose four centuries ago. I believe that St Francis would do the same, and Jesus, and the Buddha, and all who have seen the light. I can't for a single instant believe that they would have anything to learn from our way of life. The believers of this world mouth agreement, I know, but their actions speak differently. De Vaca had learned that one heals through faith, that one conquers by gentleness. 'It is curious,' he writes to His Majesty, 'when one has nobody and nothing to rely upon outside of oneself.' Yes, it is indeed curious. 'To understand what it means to have nothing one must have nothing.' True. And yet, who but a handful of men in all history have dared the experience.

The men who govern the world promise this and that, always freedom, honour, security – and work. Their promises are empty, have been proved empty again and again and again. But men who are empty like empty promises. The man who counsels, 'Look to yourself, the power is within you!' is looked upon as a dreamer and a madman. Yet these are the very men who performed miracles, who altered the world. None of them spoke of possessions, of security, of honour, or of freedom. They spoke of God and of his presence everywhere, even in the soul of the unbeliever. They spoke of the dictates of the heart, of dedication and devotion, of service to one's fellow man, of charity, of love, of tolerance and forbearance, of humility, of forgiveness. Cabeza de Vaca was one of the few men in this great hemisphere who acted upon these principles of faith. The simple story of his illumination, his irrevocable change of heart, wipes out the bloody tales of Cortés and Pizarro and of all the conquerors of the earth from time immemorial. It leads us to believe what deep in our hearts we all know, that a man can always stop dead in his tracks and, facing the truth, exemplify it in action. It leads us to believe more, that in truth nothing less than this will ever satisfy man. And this, I believe, is the meaning of the Journey which we all are making.

THE MARVELLOUS ADVENTURE
OF CABEZA DE VACA

YOUR MAJESTY,

I am that Nuñez Cabeza de Vaca who lately sent you a Relation of his shipwrecks and mischances during the eight years he was absent from your dominions. In painful doubt whether my words were clear enough, I write again. My meanings being new to Your Majesty and at a hasty glance unconcerned with your prestige, you might consider my narrative a poor occasion for exercising your serene power of understanding. The fault would then lie in me, not in what I have to say. † Be my forgiving reader, Your Majesty. Grant me your grace.

I was at the battle of Ravenna in 1512. Between dawn and sunset that day perished a thousand score. Young as I was, Ravenna taught me something of how easy to tear asunder and destroy a man is, body and spirit. In the days that followed, in my desolation first confronted with slaughter, I saw a far-off light, heard a far-off strain of music. † Such words serve as well as any: what can describe a happening in the shadows of the soul?

Again that far-off flicker of music came to me in the disorders at Sevilla in 1521, when I fought under the Duke of Medina-Sidonia.

Seven years passed without that flash of inward fire and I forgot about it. Sevilla was then a marvellous, disturbing world. I saw the heretics burning in the arms of the iron prophets. I saw Columbus as an old man, Magellan as a young man. The sailors came ashore with parrots and gold ingots and Indian girls.

Then I too sailed across the seas, Lord Treasurer of the expedition of Pámfilo Narvaez.

All that day when we were in sight of Teneriffe I thought of my grandfather, the conqueror of the Grand Canary. In my childhood I was surrounded by the natives of that island, the Guanches, whom he brought home as slaves. I listened to their vague and melancholy singing, learned to be at ease with inarticulate people.

For the money to conquer the Grand Canary, perhaps Your Majesty will remember, Pedro de Vera Mendoza had pawned to the Moor his two sons, my father and my uncle.

As I told Your Majesty in my account of that journey, never had expedition more calamities than ours. Some of our ships foundered from hurricanes in the harbours of Cuba. The others we left behind deliberately in the lagoons of Florida.

Our greatest misfortune, aside from our greed and ignorance, lay in our commander, Pámfilo Narvaez himself. † Pámfilo believed himself born under a lucky star, though nothing justified such a belief. Before Hernán Cortés he could have marched to Tenochtitlán. But he did not. When Cortés and his soldiers were richly quartered in the palaces of Montezuma, he could have replaced him in command. For that purpose was he dispatched from Havana by Velásquez. But Cortés came flying on horseback all the way to Vera Cruz, and talked Pámfilo's soldiers away from under his very nose. † Pámfilo was not without a magnetism. But he was cocksure, a braggart, and what was worse, uncertain of the line between dream and reality. He forgot that Cortés burnt his ships only after studying the jewelled emissaries of Montezuma, and becoming sure of the value of the quarry. Pámfilo had nothing to be sure of. And yet he pictured himself another Cortés, he pictured another Tenochtitlán concealed in the fronds of Florida. Having pictured these things, he was as certain that they existed as of the vein in his neck.

Your Majesty is at liberty to picture *us* under this ageing, adipose, credulous commander. Across that steaming land we marched with our armour glittering and our horses covered with gaudy trappings, 578 of us, towards utter ruin. † Believing that on the page of history we would share the glory of Cortés and his murderous band . . .

Pámfilo would summon the copper-coloured natives and tell them with gestures that he was searching for a city of the size and value of Tenochtitlán. † The Indians had never heard of Tenochtitlán nor of Montezuma. But they had heard of a big town and pointed northwards exclaiming, 'Apaláchee!'

We marched and we marched, and had fevers and fevers. Yes, Your Majesty is at liberty to picture us.

Apaláchee was no Tenochtitlán . . . We found it. It was in an immense swamp, a large impoverished settlement of thatched huts, a place of unbearable squalor.

There was nothing for it but seek the sea again and sail back to Cuba. Our arms and armour made us feel like dolts, and we wished we had pierced the jungle carrying carpenter's tools. For now, without axe, adze, or hammer, we had to build ourselves boats.

This is the tale of what men can and cannot do when they must do something or die.

We built nine open boats. During the weeks it required, some of us went with scant food, and those whose palates allowed it devoured the horses.

Our 580 men had become 400 when at last we set sail and left behind us the Indian marksmen and the snakes, neither of which in Florida err when they strike.

Day after day tide and wind washed us out to sea and then washed us in to land, along a dazzling and uncertain coast. From thirst, and from the exposure to the frightful sun, our 400 became forty.

Who knows what was lost in these boats? Another Magellan, another Camoens, another Cervantes, another St John of the Cross . . .

No one has so sympathetic an imagination as Your Majesty. You will understand what I am not telling you; that I saw men jump overboard, mad from thirst and sun. That I saw them swell and die slowly in delirium, heard their words and songs put out the pitiful contents of their minds. That I saw men gnaw at corpses. And that these were Spanish gentlemen.

It is curious to have so graphic a lesson in what life may become. We had been a proud band, relying on our united strength, our armour, and our horses. Slowly our strength disunited, until nothing that we had in common remained to help any of us.

As I say, it is curious when one has nobody and nothing to rely upon outside of oneself.

Yet again that music, that fitful run and flash of brightness I first heard on the battlefield of Ravenna. Your Majesty is renowned as a patron of music; here was a music it is possible you may never have heard.

Somewhere on that coast a handful of us crawled ashore, and were fed and tended by kindly Indians till we regathered nervous vitality for the hopeless voyage to Cuba. We stript and launched the boat, first putting our clothes aboard her. But a great comber capsized the rotten, heavy hulk, imprisoning and drowning three of us. The others emerged mother-naked on the beach, shivering in the November wind of that overcast afternoon.

The Indians came back and found us as naked as they were, and our barge gone, and in tears. They sat down beside us and cried, too. I cried all the harder, to think people so miserable had pity for us. † I have informed Your Majesty of their tears and mine. These simple Indians were the first relenting of nature to us in months and months. † That evening, for fear we might die on the way, the Indians made fires at intervals along the path to their village, warming us at each fire. That night and many nights after we slept beside them on the oyster shells which floor their huts, wrapt in hides against the cold winds from the sea.

While we were subjects of Your Majesty, we had everything life offers, and now we had nothing. To understand what it means to have nothing one must have nothing. † No clothing against the weather might appear the worst. But for us poor skeletons who survived it, it was not.

The worst lay in parting little by little with the thoughts that clothe the soul of a European, and most of all with the idea that a man attains strength through dirk and dagger, and serving in Your Majesty's guard. We had to surrender such fantasies till our inward nakedness was the nakedness of an unborn babe, starting life anew in a womb of sensations which in themselves can mysteriously nourish. Several years went by before I could relax in that living plexus for which even now I have no name; but only when at last I relaxed, could I see the possibilities of a life in which to be deprived of Europe was not to be deprived of too much.

Tempests came, we could pull no more roots from the sea-channels, the canebrake yielded no more fish. People died in the flimsy lodges. † News came that five Spaniards further down the coast, men from another barge, had eaten one another up till but one remained. This deed startled the innocence of our Indians. They debated whether to kill us, to be rid of us. Instead, they made us their beasts of burden.

In April the Indians went down to the sea, taking us with them; for a whole month we ate the black-berries of the sand dunes. The Indians danced incessantly. They asked us to cure their sick. When we said we did not know how to cure, they with-held our food from us. † We began to watch the procedure of their medicine men. It seemed to us both irreligious and uninstructed. Besides, we found the notion of healing Indians somewhat repellent, as Your Majesty will understand. † But we had to heal them or die. So we prayed for strength. We prayed on bended knees and in an agony of hunger. Then over each ailing Indian we made the sign of the Cross, and recited the Ave María and a Pater Noster. † To our amazement the ailing said they were well. And not only they but the whole tribe went without food so that we might have it. † Yet so great was the lack of food for us all, it seemed impossible that life could last.

Truly, it was to our amazement that the ailing said they were well. Being Europeans, we thought we had given away to doctors and priests our ability to heal. But here it was, still in our possession, even if we had only Indians to exercise it upon. It was ours after all, we were more than we had thought we were.

33

I am putting my words together for whatever intelligence there may be in the world. There is no other reality among men than this intelligence; Sire, it is greatly to your glory that you can incarnate it.

To be more than I thought I was – a sensation utterly new to me . . .

Starvation, nakedness, slavery: sensations utterly new to me, also . . . † The last of my fellow Spaniards on the island dies . . . † Nothing to eat after the sea-roots sprouted but the blackberries of the sand dunes. Nothing to protect me from the attack of the terrible frost, or the terrible sun. No one who knew my language . . . † And it endured for months, for years maybe . . . Everyone I saw as starved as I was. The human body emaciated, the lean cheek, the burning eye – the ribs showing, each rib distinct – the taut skin, the weak loins, the shrunken haunch and pap. † In the whole world there can be no poverty like the poverty of these people. I could not stand it. I ran away . . .

At this time, as I remember it, I began to think of Indians as fellow human beings. If I introduce this idea it is to prepare Your Majesty for other ideas which came to me later, in consequence.

These were days when I reassorted the pictures of my childhood, as a child turns his kaleidoscope. I saw the Guanche slaves anew, and as though I were one of them. I saw my grandfather through the eyes of his slaves. I remembered, now without laughing, how he had tricked the Guanches into slavery. He pretended to enlist them to sail from the Grand Canary to conquer Teneriffe, and when he had them below decks he battened down the hatches and set sail for Cádiz . . .

My grandfather's brutality earned him the public denunciation of Bishop Juan de Frías. This too I remembered.

In this wilderness I became a trader, and went to and fro on the coast and a little inland. † I went inland with seashells and cockles, and a certain shell used to cut beans, which the natives value. I came out with hides, and red ochre for the face and hair, flint for arrow-points, and tassels of deerhide. † I came to be well known among the tribes, and found out the lay of the land.

One day I heard someone calling me by name,

'Alvar Nuñez, Alvar Nuñez!' It was Alonso del Castillo, one of the captains of the expedition. He said that Pámfilo's barge had drifted ashore among unfriendly Indians, and left of its occupants were only himself and Captain Andrés Dorantes, and Dorantes' blackamoor, Estevanico. † We hid ourselves in a thicket and laid our plans.

That summer, when the coast tribes came together for the summer orgies, we four made good our escape westwards.

Thus our 580 had become 400, our 400, forty, and our forty, four.

Certain natives came to Castillo. From ribs to cleft they were having spasms, and they begged him to cure them. He prayed, and required us anxiously to pray with him. When he had done praying he made the sign of the Cross over the Indians, and their spasms left off. † We knelt down to give thanks for this new amazement.

Through this region there are no trails, and I lost my way. I found a burning tree to spend that very cold night beside. In the morning I loaded myself with dry wood, and took two burning sticks. Thus with fuel and fire, I went on for five days, seeing nobody, but having the sun with me by day and Mazzaroth and Arcturus by night. † These five days I felt a numbness of those organs which keep one aware of the misery of existence. † When curing sick Indians, I have struggled to shut out the thought of Andrés and Alonso (for we are self-conscious, knowing one another's sins); and in the effort of praying I have felt as though something in me had broken, to give me the power of healing. But alone in this wilderness no tissue of the body hindered the mysterious power.

Nothing of me, Your Majesty, existed then outside of that music I first heard at Ravenna.

The sixth day I found my companions, who had concluded that a snake must have bitten me. † I told them we ought not to be self-conscious with one another. That power we had felt flowing in us and through us could not, in the nature of things, be acutely conscious of us as individuals. It must come rather as wind comes to the trees of a forest, or as the ocean continues to murmur in the seashell it has thrown ashore.

A gulf deeper than ocean yawns between the old

world and the new; and what by now I was accustomed to, would startle a burgher of Madrid or of Salamanca.

At Sevilla in my youth, as I have said, I saw the heretics burning in the arms of the iron prophets. This picture was with me often. Perhaps, like me, those heretics had had to pick up their notions of the Invisible as they went through life, and without the assistance of book or priest. What I myself was learning, came from many blinding days in an open boat, while men died beside me crying for their mothers; and from living among these simple Indians, who insisted on our curing them of their ills. And so my notions of the Invisible may differ from what the books say. I mention it in passing, Your Majesty.

When he assailed my grandfather openly in his cathedral, calling him coward and fiend, did Juan de Frías follow a lesson he had learned by rote? That good bishop had a heart and mind to which life itself could speak, and speak forcibly.

Indians came bringing five persons shrivelled and paralysed and very ill. Each of the five offered Castillo silently his bows and arrows. Castillo prayed, we with him; in the morning the five were cured . . .

Indians came from many places. But Castillo was always afraid his sins would interfere with his working miracles. The Indians turned to me. I told Castillo it was no moment for indulging the idea of being sinful, and then I followed the Indians to their ranch. † The dying man was dead; Dorantes and I found him with eyes upturned, and no pulse. I removed the mat that covered him and prayed. At last the something in me like a membrane broke, and I was confident the old man would rise up again. As he did. During the night the natives came to tell us he had talked, eaten and walked about. They gave us many presents, and we left them the happiest people on earth, for they had given away their very best.

Your Majesty may by now have had enough of our cures and curing, exertions outside of Holy Church, and for the sole benefit of miserable Indians. Yet so profound is your courtesy, I know, that you will let me reveal all that is within my heart. † We found ourselves so pressed that Dorantes and the Moor, who had little taste for it, had to become medicine men, too. † Boys and girls, men and women, old men and women, human bodies deformed, starved, wasted by affliction (only rarely one sound and firm) . . . † Their eyes followed us every moment. I do not forget those eyes . . . † Your Majesty, since I addressed you first, you have become more mysterious to me and more majestic, and this increases my sense of freedom in speaking to you. To the understanding of such days and events this additional narrative becomes necessary, like a real figure to walk beside a ghost. † Those eyes . . . they thrust me out of myself, into a world where nothing, if done for another, seems impossible.

Months went by as in a dream. The nerve of vision no longer rendered plausible that European world of which we had been a part. That world grew fantastic, and fantastic our countrymen there. † We ourselves were only too real. From lack of clothing we had big sores and deep skin fissures on our backs and shoulders, and it hurt us to carry the hides we slept in. And it hurt us to find firewood among the cactus. My thighs and arms bled so much I stood it only by remembering – and yet whom or what did I remember? Was it a person – was it a quality of life – was it an emotion? Was it even a remembering, was it not perhaps a listening?

Often for a time it rained gently at dusk, soothing

our thighs and arms. In one such dusk we en-countered squinting women in an opening. They were afraid to run away from the three pale figures and the shadowy blackamoor, for they us took to be gods floating about in the mist and rain. † They led us to a village of fifty huts. Here we cured, and cured . . .

Our journey westward was but a long series of en-counters. Your Majesty, encounters have become my meditation. † The moment one accosts a stranger or is accosted by him is above all in this life the moment of drama. The eyes of Indians who crossed my trail have searched me to the very depths to estimate my *power*. † It is true the world over. It is true of a Spaniard meeting another on the road between Toledo and Salamanca. Whoever we meet watches us intently at the quick, strange moment of meeting, to see whether we are disposed to be friendly.

Seeing our bodies, seeing my own, and Alonso's, and Andrés's, and the black Moor's, sometimes I think how once I was different, and we all were. † What would Doña Alonza Maldonado and her hus-band Dr Castillo of Salamanca think, if they could see their little boy Alonso today, striding here ahead of me, lashed by starvation, scorched and baked by the sun, his hair and beard unkempt, small about the flanks, his body shrivelled like a mummy?

In youth the human body drew me and was the object of my secret and natural dreams. † But body after body has taken away from me that sensual phosphorescence which my youth delighted in. Within me is no disturbing interplay now, but only the steady currents of adaptation and of sympathy.

Your Majesty's piercing mind glides pliantly through what is interstitial and hidden. † But upon me it was dawning only slowly that I had it in my discretion to grant life and health to others ... † Imagine me then perturbed; you are aware of what my training had been as one of Your Majesty's soldiers.

Dark clouds rise to the south. † To the west a great rainbow spreads its double arc. Alonso strides sturdily towards it. After him comes the Arab Negro from Azamor, whose black limbs endure every privation and still shine with superfluous sweat. For this blackamoor am I specially grateful. His reflections on our suffering do not reduce him to apathy. No adverse heats and chills deprive his loins of their strength. He is a sight to see, carrying a copper rattle in his hand, and on his shoulder a green and orange parrot.

There was the afternoon we crossed a big river, more than waist deep, as wide as the Guadalquivir at Sevilla, and with a swift current. I speak of it again because I loved it.

There was the village where each Indian wished to be the first to touch us, and we were squeezed almost to death in the sweating crowd . . .

. . . the village so solicitous to be blest that Alonso fainted of exhaustion . . .

. . . the village where a new custom began: the Indians who came with us took from the villagers all their bows, arrows, shoes and beads. From that time on, those who accompanied us took tribute of those to whom they brought us. It made us uneasy, but the victims reassured us. They said they were too glad to see us to feel the loss of their property – and besides, they could make good their losses at the next village, who were very rich Indians . . .

*   *   *

. . . the plain where first we saw mountains, very
low, like white sheep lying down . . .

. . . the village where they were so pertinacious
about touching us all over that in three hours we
could not get through with them . . .

. . . the village where many had one eye clouded,
and others were totally blind from the same cause:
which amazed us . . .

To clarify the same occurrences, words can be
arranged differently, as no one knows better than
Your Majesty. † It was a drunkenness, this feeling
I began to have of power to render life and happiness to others. Yet I was concerned about it. The
concern was the important thing – not the wonder-
ing about the nature of the power, how widespread
it might be, how deep, whether Andrés or Alonso or
Estevanico had it in equal measure with me. † What
occupied me was whether I myself knew how to use
it, whether I could master it, whether indeed it was
for me to master – perhaps being a self-directing
power that came through me. † But after one accus-
toms oneself to the idea, it is good to be able to
give out health and joy whether one man have it, or
whether we all have it. Had this thought occurred to

44

Your Majesty? Never before had it occurred to me.

I said to Andrés, 'If we reach Spain I shall petition His Majesty to return me to this land, with a troop of soldiers. And I shall teach the world how to conquer by gentleness, not by slaughter.' †
'Why then a troop of soldiers?' asked Dorantes, smiling. 'Soldiers look for Indian girls and gold.'
† 'Perhaps I could teach them otherwise.' † 'They would kill you, or tie you to a tree and leave you. What a dunce you are, Alvar Nuñez!'

'And what will *you* do if we reach Spain again?' I asked Andrés. † 'It will be enough to reach Mexico,' he answered. 'I may look about for a rich widow, and spend the rest of my life as a rancher.' †
'I could not care for such a life,' I said. † 'To each his adventure,' replied Andrés.

It occurred to me that Andrés might be afraid of the great power at this period within us. I inquired of him. 'Yes, I am afraid – who would not be?' he answered, earnestly.

Another day, after he had been silent a long time, Andrés said to us: † 'If I could always heal these people and help them, I might be willing to stay

among them. I don't know. But our present relation to them is caused by our novelty, our transi-
ency, and the surprise at our good works. That state
of things would wear off. † Besides, it is not miracles
these people need. They need everything fate has
stript us of in bringing us amongst them naked and
on equal terms. Yet not quite equal. We can remember childhood and youth in a land where people
live in stone houses, till the same fields year after
year, build barns to store the harvests in. The towns
are related to one another and support the mutual
good. Each nobleman and alcalde is an avenue
leading to the king; and king, alcalde, thief, and
villager all bow to the will of God through Holy
Church.'

I take my time thinking these words over. They are
true and yet I cannot assent to them. Then I
answer Andrés: † 'When these Indians call upon
us to have mercy and heal them, is the power they
feel in us derived from stone houses, barns and
tilled fields – from alcalde or nobleman, or from
Holy Church, for that matter? Let the truth be
said, Andrés: all that we learned across the water
we have had to throw away. Only what we learned
as babes in our mothers' arms has stayed with us to
help others.' † 'And what did we learn in our

mothers' arms, good dunce?' asked Andrés, putting his arm around my shoulder.

. . . a mountain seven leagues long, the stones of which were iron slags . . .

. . . a night when the moon was round, and in its light a multitude of dwellings beside an unexpected and charming river . . .

. . . a man who some years since had been shot through the left side of the back with an arrow. He told me the wound made him feel sick all the while. I observed that the head of the arrow lay in the cartilage. I prayed for an hour, and then grasped the very sharp, thin stone which served me as a knife, and cut open the breast. Feeling for the arrowhead, I thrust my hand into the palpitating tissue of the body. Your Majesty, that we human beings should be made of limp, wet meat appeared to me as strange as that we should be also air and spirit; and in that hour nausea and a quick curiosity mingled with my pity . . .

This cure was a misfortune to us; it gained us fame in every direction. We soon had with us three or four thousand persons. It went past human endurance to breathe on and make the sign of the

Cross over every morsel they ate. In these parts mountain deer, quail, birds, rabbits abounded, and what they killed the Indians set before us. They would not touch it and would have died of hunger had we not yielded the blessing they asked for. Besides, they asked our permission for various things they felt like doing, and it soon wore us out. † Even doing good, it appears, can lead to ennui, even the sight of the happiness one causes can satiate. † And yet Your Majesty will rejoice that heaven vouchsafed us a weariness such as this, perhaps never before experienced by a European.

Tribe after tribe, language after language . . . nobody's memory could recall them all. Always they robbed one another, but those who lost and those who gained were equally content.

Estevanico, the good black, the good link between the aloofness of white men and the warm spermatic life of the Indians. Men, women and children joked and played with him. What matter what he did, he was not wearied of it. What matter what he did, the mystery failed not to act through him to heal and restore.

. . . fifty leagues through a land of desert, with nothing to eat and little to drink. Through villages where the women dressed in white deerskin and people lived in real houses . . . people the best formed we had seen, the liveliest and most capable, and those who best understood us . . .

. . . moonlight in another adobe village, and we four alternately standing or lying down in the centre of the plaza, and the Indians running to us from all the houses with gifts, touching us and running back to their houses for more gifts, running to us again and touching us – a living, glistening cobweb of runners in the moon – keeping up for hours this naked flash to and fro from centre to periphery, periphery to centre.

Your Majesty, such were the scenes in which I found myself treating all human beings alike. I screw up my courage to confess it. † Perhaps it is the secret thing which life has it in itself to become – a long, long march on the road, meeting people, thrown into relations with them, having to meet demands often terrible and, without the aid of mysterious power, impossible: demands of healing and understanding, and constantly the exorcism of fear.

*   *   *

With a reasonable man and a timorous man and a carnal man as my companions, and even part of me. And who is any of us, that without starvation he can go through the kingdoms of starvation?

And seventeen successive days of starvation.

And a sunset, on a plain between very high mountains, with a people who for four months of the year eat only powdered straw . . .

And more starvation . . .

And permanent houses once more, where maize is harvested, and where they gave us brightly decorated blankets. † For a hundred leagues good houses and harvested crops, the women better treated than anywhere else. They wear shoes, and blouses open in front and tied with deer string. † At sunrise these people lift their clasped hands to the horizon and pass them over their bodies. At sunset they repeat the gesture. As I watched them at these devotions, I recalled a youngster from Cádiz, one of those who died of thirst beside me in the open boat. That boy drank in the beauty of Florida, watched palm and headland along the coast even in his final delirium. I was sorry he had not lived on to see these natives laving their golden figures in the gold of dawn.

*　　　*　　　*

At last we found a sign of our countrymen – what through years and years we had been praying for. †
On the neck of an Indian a little silver buckle from a sword belt, with a horseshoe nail sewed inside it ... We questioned him. He said that men with beards like ours had come from heaven to that river; that they had horses, lances, and swords, and had lanced two Indians.

The country grew more and more doleful. The natives had fled to the mountains, leaving their fields. The land was fertile and full of streams, but the people were wan. They told us our countrymen had burnt all the villages, taking with them half the men and all the women and children ...

Then a day when Indians said that on the night before they had watched the Christians from behind some trees. They saw them take along many persons in chains.

Our countrymen, these slave-catchers, were startled when they saw us approaching. Yet almost with their first words they began to recite their troubles. For many days they had been unable to find Indians to capture. They did not know what to do, and were on the point of starvation. † The idea of enslaving our

Indians occurred to them in due course, and they were vexed at us for preventing it. They had their interpreter make a fine speech. He told our Indians that we were as a matter of fact Christians too, but had gone astray for a long while, and were people of no luck and little heart. But the Christians on horseback were real Christians, and the lords of the land to be obeyed and served. † Our Indians considered this point of view. They answered that the real Christians apparently lied, that we could not possibly be Christians. For we appeared out of sunrise, they out of sunset; we cured the sick, while they killed even the healthy; we went naked and barefoot, while they wore clothes and rode horseback and stuck people with lances; we asked for nothing and gave away all we were given, while they never gave anybody anything and had no other aim than to steal.

Your Majesty will remember my indignation in my first narrative, that Christians should be so wicked, especially such as had the advantages of being your subjects. † I did not at the time understand the true source of my indignation. I do now, and I will explain it. In facing these marauders I was compelled to face the Spanish gentleman I myself had been eight years before. It was not easy to think of it.

Andrés and Alonso agreed that it was not easy. †
What, Your Majesty, is so melancholy as to confront
one's former unthinking and unfeeling self?

It was many days before I could endure the touch
of clothing, many a night before I could sleep in a
bed.

Shoes were the worst. In the Spanish settlements I
dared not go barefoot, for provincials are the most
easily shocked of Spaniards. I had not valued
enough the pressure of earth on my naked feet,
while permitted that refreshment.

At first I did not notice other ways in which our
ancient civilization was affecting me. Yet soon I
observed a certain reluctance in me to do good to
others. I would say to myself, Need I exert what is
left of me, I who have undergone tortures in an
open boat and every privation and humiliation
among the Indians, when there are strong, healthy
men about me, fresh from Holy Church and from
school, who know their Christian duty? † We
Europeans all talk this way to ourselves. It has
become second nature to us. Each nobleman and
alcalde and villager is an avenue that leads us to this
way of talking; we can admit it privately, Your

Majesty, can we not? If a man need a cloak, we do not give it to him if we have our wits about us; nor are we to be caught stretching out our finger in aid of a miserable woman. Someone else will do it, we say. Our communal life dries up our milk: we are barren as the fields of Castile. We regard our native land as a power which acts of itself, and relieves us each of exertion. † While with them I thought only about doing the Indians good. But back among my fellow countrymen, I had to be on my guard not to do them positive harm. If one lives where all suffer and starve, one acts on one's own impulse to help. But where plenty abounds, we surrender our generosity, believing that our country replaces us each and several. † This is not so, and indeed a delusion. On the contrary, the power of maintaining life in others lives within each of us, and from each of us does it recede when unused. It is a concentrated power. If you are not acquainted with it, Your Majesty can have no inkling of what it is like, what it pretends, or the ways in which it slips from one. † In the name of God,

Your Majesty,

FAREWELL

MALINCHE
(Doña Marina)

Gratefully to
ERNA FERGUSSON
who first acquainted me
with Malinche

She who speaks to you out of her heaven is that Malinche whom Hernán Cortés called Marina. When my father the cacique of Oluta died, I being eight years, my mother sold me to Tabascan slave traders to secure the inheritance for my half-brother. Yet this was the deed of that destiny which from my birth has kept me in the path for me to follow.

We the disinherited sit quietly in the mossy smell of the great forest. Like me, these old men are slaves.

One has running sores from his daily burden.

'Are the sores better?' I whisper. We whisper always for fear of spying priests.

He will not let me anoint his wounds. He is like too many people, he wishes to die.

But the old man who shares my soul does not

59

wish to die. He remembers what it was my father taught us:

'The God with the cornsilk hair remains. The Feathered Serpent remains.'

The naked boys play by the wide river. Through a gigantic cedar hung with vines comes an aromatic breeze, moist, and frank with the mystery of wild love. I am picking berries where great moths flutter in the late-slanted sun.

The young Icac comes down the river path from his hunting. Like still water, woman receives the image of a man. Thus I receive Icac, and his sadness is not the great sadness of sex, filled with confusion and melancholy.

'Icac, you are a closed flower, like me, swaying heavily all day from stem to stem. Yet at night I open to the stars. I take the Feathered Serpent to my heart, and pray.'

'The Feathered Serpent is a dream medicine, Malinche, and if you have it you can cure yourself; but you cannot cure others. As for me, I peer into the future, and I find for ever priests and soldiers wasting our children and ourselves. The whole earth is a grave and nothing escapes it. We cannot go our own way any more, we are filled with bad thoughts.'

I say to Icac, 'Do not talk the way people talk who are afraid, and huddle in the dark.'

When I was a child, my old nurse told me endless stories about how people come up out of the earth, and when they have come up go around on the earth everywhere, and live and grow old.

'If you do your own way, the earth will push you off,' she would say to me. 'These things were told to us when the earth was made. You must not remember what you have in your own head. It is better to sing to the river and the trees, "My father, I want to be your daughter. I want you to give me all you can. I want you to put good thoughts in my head." '

This morning at the well I saw my old nurse and said to her: 'I want to know what is best for me to do.'

She said, 'You must find out whether there is anything better to do than to take care of people.'

My eyes blur looking at my old nurse. She is a Mayan idol, calm and sacred.

When one is eighteen, one should never be sad in an ancient world of great trees and lake-like rivers and gay parrots. But when old and young, rich and poor, forget the Feathered Serpent and find no way back into the earth they were made of, what is one to do?

The village is suddenly excited. The men of Cintla talk to one another, boys talk to boys, women to women.

White men have landed on the coast.

I too am excited.

The Feathered Serpent, the White God, has kept his word and returned to us.

I want my country to grow, to be fine enough for all who ever come to it.

I rise and begin dancing without knowing why.

It is not to be dreamt of that my countrymen can overcome the White God. But they will fight, and when they are conquered, they will have to give him girls and gold.

I am not good enough, but, O newly returned White God, I shall die if I am not among the presents given you.

What are you whom I love? To what warmth do I nestle?

Now I begin to know why I am dancing.

(25 March 1519)

The newcomers make gestures. Their movements are quick. They wear outlandish garments that do not smell like flowers.

They carry sticks that shoot fire, and a few of them ride gentle-eyed, ungainly beasts called horses. My countrymen did not overcome them, and so they must give them gold and girls. I am happy, I am to be one of the girls.

Concerning me in particular the caciques speak to the White Gods. They say that I am a present worth much gold, many maidens; I have been taught the mysteries of things, and can speak many languages.

The White God is called Hernán Cortés. From his horse he looks at me intently, and my knees shake. He has deep shadows under his eyes. He is different from all other men, but I do not know why.

The White God divides us among certain soldiers. Me he honours, he gives me to his friend, Alonso Puertocarrero, who stands close beside him.

As I fall asleep that night I see my nurse's face. Nurse seems about to say something to me, something she can never say, for I am in another world, I am in this world now, and there is no time.

The sea is a dusk-deep lazuli.

We sail along the shore in big boats. Five Cintla girls are aboard with me, and they are unhappy. They are afraid to be in a strange world with such powerful men. I say to them:

'Is it a time to be happy or unhappy? Tell the sea what you are thinking. Hold up your right hand and talk to the sea. Everything will hear you and understand you, and good thoughts will go into your hearts.

'If Quetzalcoatl came as a scorpion, as a vulture, as a wild pig, should we not receive him? Yet these are handsome young men – he whom they call Alvarado is golden as the sun. Surely for a good purpose did the spirits cause our people to give us to these persons. Our country must be large and wide enough for the White God who returns to us.'

My lot is to take care of people, and also of sick and despairing people. What Nurse said is true. I ask the wounded soldiers to teach me words from their language. Today they taught me their important words, those that mean fever and blood and pus and death, and gold and money and fear, and haste and worry, and nightmare and prayer and mother and Mother of God.

The dawn this morning is a million water lilies in the sky, and when the sun ascends, the sea is alive with rosy, laughing lips.

Cortés has a man named Aguilár, who was shipwrecked and has lived in Yucatan, and knows our language. Today Cortés talked with me through this man. Aguilár can speak Castilian and the language of Yucatan; but I speak languages he never heard of. I am excited, I see that if I learn my lord's language, I can become his interpreter.

Today I learned many names for things from the wounded soldiers, and also from Puertocarrero (who does not teach me for nothing). If I am to serve my lord, I must prepare the bride. If I am woman, I must be the interpreter.

When I think such things I am so happy that I hear at a great distance. I think I can hear all over the world.

Canoes put out from the beach when we anchor in the bay, and brown bodies climb aboard. Hernán Cortés goes ashore to talk with the masters of these Indians. We can see them: they are richly dressed persons and stand proudly.

Inside me a pair of eyes is observing everyone and everything. And nerves of the earth come to life in me and speak too. These men of Spain know too little. You must not pray directly for what you want. You must pray that everything is the way it should be between what is inside you and what is outside you. Then you will have good harvests and good children. How can these men be gods? How can they be bringing my country good? I bear a confused suffering in my heart.

Tonight the sunset was blood on a black wall.

Cortés is going to Montezuma, to the great city of Tenochtitlán. I am glad, but he does not know that the land of Tlascala lies between him and Montezuma.

The forests are dark as purple pansies, tangled with tree-ferns and orchids. Through one empty pueblo after another we march inland. Human sacrifices lie on the altars, freshly slain by the people, who are afraid.

The white men shrink from these sights. They too are afraid.

Today, on an altar beneath a great pink-flowering locust, I saw the mutilated body of a boy. The priests had taken out his heart and sawed off one of his arms. Blood was clotted in his blue-black hair. He had a beautiful face; what was left of him had still the beauty of the brown boys of the pueblos.

His sightless eyes stay with me, as though he had something in his mind to say. But I am in a world now where there is no time either to speak or to understand.

It was Cortés who gave the grey mare to Alonso.

He bought it with gold knots off his velvet cloak, the day before they sailed from Cuba.

And Alonso says that a short while before they sailed Cortés took to himself a bride. Her name is Catalina, and she waits for him in Cuba. But why does she wait for him in Cuba, why is she not here, marching towards Montezuma beside his horse, like me?

I go off by myself and pray. I pray the spirits to look through me and see what kind of girl I am, whether I am fit to be assisted.

Cortés rules with words and gestures. When he calls his men together and speaks to them, the fox is in him, the eagle is in him. So too is the gay parrot, and the snake without eyelids. He has great power, and there is no other man like him. Maybe he is not a man, maybe he is a Person.

Sometimes in camp, as in a dream, I find myself walking towards Cortés, only to be near him. He observes it. He makes occasions to speak with me. He asks me to repeat what I know of the God with cornsilk hair.

I must still reach him through Aguilár. I tell him, 'The Good God came to our ancestors full grown, like you. He was white, and he had a beard, like you. His words stay in my heart, for my father told me them: "Offer only lovely things on my altars," he said; "the bread of life, and jewels and feathers, and flowers. Let the streams of life flow in peace. Turn from violence. Learn to think for a long time how to change this world, how to make it better to live in. All the people in the world ought to talk about it and speak well of it, always. Then it will last for ever, and the flowers will bloom for ever. And I will come to you again." '

Cortés is no longer nervous and restless when I tell him of the Person he is supposed to embody. He rubs his beard slowly and thinks about things.

Cortés is to dispatch Alonso Puertocarrero across the water on an errand to the great Emperor. He has been giving Alonso gold; two days ago he gave him also the beautiful daughter of the great cacique Cuesco, who has been baptized Doña Francesca. I am not to go to Spain with Alonso, and I am glad. With him, one girl is as good as another. And now Cortés bids him goodbye, and Alonso goes over the sea, with the gold and the princess.

The white men quarrel every day. Some of them hate Cortés, some fear the governor of Cuba and think Cortés does wrong to disobey him and not return. Some have tried to desert, and Cortés has hanged two of them.

To end the discontent, Cortés sends word to the coast to burn all the ships but one.

Now there is no way to go back. The men must go ahead, as Cortés wishes.

His gods are helping him. He would not dare burn the ships otherwise. I know now what his gods are: they are the Virgin and the Babe. He would not amount to much if they were not helping him. He admits as much himself every morning and every evening, on his knees.

I am of constant service to Cortés. He needs me beside him by day; by night he rests in my arms. Love is teaching me his language quickly; and for this I thank the Virgin and the Babe, and I thank my own God too, the Feathered Quetzalcoatl.

We are resting in a pueblo called Cempoala, where the people are kind and give us food.

Today five of Montezuma's tax-collectors come to this place, walking with crooked sticks. They are arrogant and virile men with blue loin-cloths, and jewelled cloaks.

Because the Cempoalans have received us kindly though we are strangers, the tax-collectors demand twenty of their girls and boys for sacrifice.

The caciques of the pueblo are soft and yielding.

But Cortés whips them with words. He tells them to throw the tax-collectors in jail. Cortés and his emperor across the sea promise to protect Cempoala against Montezuma.

Today Cortés wrote the great Montezuma a letter not to sacrifice his subjects alive, but to kneel down and pray to the Emperor of Spain and to Our Lady the Virgin, so that the moment of his terrible anguish will not come upon him.

Daily, because of what I tell him of Quetzal-coatl, Cortés grows more wonderful.

When he acts so bravely, then most of all am I a bush which has been withering in the desert, but but now the arroyos run full and the roots jet water into the hot foliage.

Whatever Cortés says to my people reaches them through my lips. Whatever they say to him reaches him through my lips. I am my lord's mouthpiece and I am the mouthpiece of my earth.

He looks at me at times as though words were struggling on his lips which he needs to give tongue to. And yet he cannot, for there is no time.

And now Cortés has made the timid Cempoalans promise to abandon their idols. The Cempoalan priests tear their beards and prophesy evil, but the soldiers bear the idols out of the temples and grind them to powder. We whitewash the blood-stained walls, and place in the temple the image of the mild Mother and Child.

Padre de la Merced says the mass.

But the padre, who is wise, warns Cortés privately not to act by force in religious matters.

The Cempoalans lure us to attack the Cingapacingans, saying they are thieves and robbers.

It is a pretext by which they hope to rob the pueblo of Cingapacinga to the bone.

I make it clear to Cortés.

He is a righteous judge. He causes the thefts to be made good.

He causes peace to come between the two pueblos.

I am happy.

At Cempoala in the moonlight tonight I hold Cortés's hand and look at his fingers. They are like the slender fibrous stalks of a flower which grows along the wide river at home. They have arisen out of the endless past of an alien race through many moons and waters, for a girl of Mexico and for her country.

O my country, at first you will not know how to give this lover your best, nor will he know how to take your best from you. You will try him with hatred and bloodshed, but you will only rouse him the more. Shudder is to follow shudder.

This is a lover who will wait ages, who will need to wait ages, to give you all of himself.

Cortés has me borne in a litter; he gives me jewels and feathers. He tells his page to attend me, Juan de Salasar, who is younger even than I.

It is like a dream to trouble me, when all I desire is to be nameless as the earth.

No doubt Cortés loves me. But without me he could not succeed, and he knows it only too well. I am sad.

Words can be disguises. Many words Cortés uses to me are disguises. They are for a purpose, not for love.

Cortés says things and does things which do not fit him, which are horrible.

Today for the sake of discipline he cut off the left hand of one of his own soldiers.

Our deeds disguise us. People need endless time to try on their deeds, until each knows the proper deeds for him to do. But every day, every hour, rushes by. There is no time.

Yet if I were never to see this Cortés again, I should be sure his heart and mine had understood each other. Like all men, he is two men: the man he really is, and the man he would like to be.

For support, I fall back on my heart. Has a man any fault a woman cannot weave with and try to change into something better, if the god her man prays to is a mother holding a baby?

Cortés and Alvarado, Morla and León are shocked by the masks of our gods. Like frightened hens, they scuttle back to thoughts of the Virgin. But the Virgin, holding the Child, belongs to another world than theirs, and lives for those who know suffering and sadness, as these young men do not. I am building up within me a new life, apart from Cortés and Alvarado and all of them, but not apart from Quetzalcoatl, not apart from the Virgin and the Child.

Day by day we climb up from the thick forest and the moths and the dampness to a land I have always heard of: of red earth and scant trees and little rain, and three sky-reaching mountains crested with what they call snow.

And so we stand at last before Tlascala.

The brave Tlascalans will not let the Spaniards pass. They believe that Cortés is a friend of Montezuma. They hate Montezuma, and they have reason to.

In the fighting today they cut the head off the mare of Pedro de Morón, and ten Spaniards were wounded saving Morón and the saddle.

The white men are aghast at Indians who are not afraid of horses. We Indians know that the Tlascalans are afraid of nothing, not even of Montezuma.

Padre de la Merced and Juan Díaz the priest spend the whole night commending the captains and the soldiers to God, hearing them repent of sin, praying God to pardon them and save them from defeat.

On New Year's Day each year we Mexicans light the sacred fire on the naked chest of a Mexican chief, and he never murmurs. The bravery of a Spaniard is different. It goes forward in whining and tears, but it goes forward.

If Xicotenga, the high lord of Tlascala, insists on fighting, the Spaniards have little hope. Three battles have made Cortés sure of it. Xicotenga sends back the same message all the while: 'We belong to this earth. We were made when this earth was made. Why do you bother us? What kind of people do you think we are?'

My heart is drawn to Xicotenga. Could I but see and talk with him, I would explain that Cortés is no friend of Montezuma.

Xicotenga is old and blind. He would understand me: the blind know more than those who see. My heart goes out to him also because on his banner is a large white bird, with wings outstretched as though it wished to fly.

It was to such a man that Cortés dared send as a peace offering a red Flemish hat with a fluffy feather.

Tonight after the battle we count our dead. Out of fewer than twenty score, forty-five men have gone from the bright world.

The Tlascalans must not know that Spaniards can die. Cortés orders the bodies hidden in an underground house.

Twelve Spaniards are ill with disease or chills. Cortés himself burns with fever, and so does the Padre de la Merced. Most of the soldiers are wounded, some with two or more wounds; many have a continual diarrhoea; they are clothed in rags, and at night the cold wind from the mountains almost makes them perish.

My servitude as woman is to follow; but now Cortés shrinks from the man's servitude of leading. He asks my advice, keeps asking it; his masculine will has spent itself. It is the moment a woman does well to fear; but I can hear at a great distance, I can hear all over the world, and I tell my lord what is in my heart:

'Free all the Tlascalan prisoners. Keep freeing them. Keep sending them back to Xicotenga with messages of brotherliness. Tell Xicotenga you will pardon all, even the death of Morón's mare, if he will make peace and embrace you.'

Sleepless nights, and the soldiers calling on their mothers, and on the Mother of God – yes, and on me too – lying there in their blood and ordure, calling 'Doña Marina, Doña Marina'. Juan the page goes by my side all the night. I speak to every messenger and every returning prisoner, speak words to catch the attention of a man old and wise.

'To the blind man who sees in the dark, to the great chieftain who is a white bird wishful of flying, say for Malinche, Cortés's slave girl, that it is best to make peace at once, for these men are demons full of restless, quickly burning love. What harm have they done to Tlascala, that Tlascala will not let them pass on to their reckoning with Montezuma?'

*   *   *

Of the Spaniards the Padre de la Merced has done the best with himself. He searches neither gold nor girls, neither power nor excitement nor food. He knows that to be is better than to have.

I think of him with thanksgiving, for in him the body person is the same as the mind and heart person.

I have never been so happy. I have never had such demands made upon my love.

Cortés is discovering a new country, but I am discovering myself.

(25 September 1519)

The long fight over, and face to face with the great lord of Tlascala, I say today, 'Till one be sure, can one receive the Stranger? You have not been sure, Xicotenga; be sure now, as I am.'

Xicotenga nods his head.

'I would not amount to much if I did not do what the spirits tell me to do,' he says.

'I have knocked Cortés down and he has risen and gone on. I have knocked him down again, and a third and fourth time, and he has risen and gone on.

'He is no ordinary man. An ordinary man stays down when I knock him down. As one makes oneself a dwelling of adobe bricks, so Cortés heaps

77

dead body on dead body to make himself a destiny.

'This shows that he is also a bad man. But all war captains and caciques who think of themselves are bad. The good part of Cortés is that he is no ordinary man. When a bad man is also an ordinary man, the spirits are not dreaming their dreams through him, and it is well to kill him quickly and forget him. I do not kill Cortés because I do not cross the spirits. Those persons are weary of the long time it takes Montezuma to grow old, and they are sending his death to him.'

I tell Xicotenga I want the world to last for ever, and all the people to speak well of it always. But I say that Cortés makes me suffer.

Xicotenga nods his head.

'He is like a man on the outside of life, looking in,' I continue. 'He is like a man who cannot see in the dark because he will not wait until his eye adjusts itself to the lack of outward light.

'The shadow of a fern does not interest him; nor does he pick up a blue pebble, to look at it more closely, nor pass his fingers over the bark of a tree. Only what can be of use to him will he stay for. Me he loves because I am of use to him, and this is a torture. Am I not a person?'

'If he were a man a woman could love completely,' says Xicotenga, 'Cortes would not be the man to destroy the Aztec. But it is good even so for young men and young women to live with each other. The man-spirit is to the woman-spirit as a thing that lives calling to a thing that lives, and one has to love all things that are real. Accepting Cortés thus, you accept his man-spirit, and have done no evil. Each spirit goes its own way, but both will live always.

'What has a woman to give the man she follows? Her love. Her love is a spring that knows no ceasing.'

So speaks Xicotenga, each word to be weighed. But I cannot forget the images that are also Cortés: the way he mounts his horse; the way he draws his gauntleted hand down his arm from his shoulder, to the elbow, and then to the wrist, watching one with his unfathomable eye; the way he smiles through his black frown; the way he turns to me in his sleep. Such images are most of all his reality, for thus he lives in my heart and memory.

Without the friendship of Tlascala we should all be dead. Today the high chieftains, to seal this friendship, bring their daughters to Cortés.

Xicotenga's daughter is to be baptized and called

Doña Luisa, and Cortés will give her in marriage to blond Pedro de Alvarado. The daughter of the cacique Mase Escasi, a beauty in ten thousand, is to be baptized Doña Elvira and Juan Velásquez de León is to have her.

Xicotenga has ordered one thousand picked warriors to attend the princesses on the march against Montezuma.

Cholula – where once the Cornsilk God lived and taught people to think how to make this world a better place to live in – Cholula, where now each year they sacrifice countless victims on countless altars.

Cholula the treacherous.

The wife of a Cholulan says to me, 'Tomorrow we slay your lord and his soldiers. Come home with me – why should you die? You can marry my son.'

I pretend to collect my clothes to go with her; leaving the chamber, I seek out Cortés, and repeat her words.

It is the last morning, the answer of Cortés to treachery . . .

My lord summons the priests and caciques and they fill the courtyard of his quarters.

The locked gates, the slaughter. The thorough

slaughter extending into the streets, man after man, child after child: a dozen, a hundred, a thousand – how many? Who knows. Who will ever know. I grieve for the Cholulans.

Before they died they said it was at Montezuma's orders they did what they did.

An Indian comes to me secretly today, saying that Escalante and the men we left behind us at Vera Cruz are murdered. I am to tell Cortés. I tell him. He says, 'Let nobody know.' He draws a deep breath and goes into his inward chamber, closing the door upon him.

(8 November 1519)

Tenochtitlán ... It is a landscape of water and islands; it is like my native Tabasco and the great rivers.

Water is beautiful and the flowers that bloom upon it and beside it.

The rivers and swamps of my country have no such far vistas as one sees here; but they are more mysterious. Tenochtitlán is not a city sprung out of the earth itself. It was built on trees driven into mud by the Aztecs who conquered the country, and who are now to be conquered in their turn.

In the air one breathes always the smell of blood.

*   *   *

81

I lie awake, listening. Cortés walks to and fro in the chamber.

Day and night he sweats with fever. He sees no way out. He trusts no one.

Yet he has a source of strength beyond life. The nervous pacing ceases. He is on his knees – he prays to the mild Mother and the Child.

Today Montezuma escorted Cortés to the temple. Now Cortés has returned.

'It had the stench of a slaughter-house in Spain,' he told me. 'Alvarado said so, too. The butterfly-god of war had five hearts on his altar, fresh, almost quivering. The walls were clotted. It was a thing to see.'

His face was greenish, but he vomited and felt better, and went on:

'It seems they call the captives kept for sacrifice *those destined to a flowery death*, and the women doomed to the gods of the mountains *those who care for flowers*. It is pretty, is it not, Chiquita? ...

'They have great delicacy. They call the battle-field *the place where the jewels are destroyed, where the lovely emeralds are broken into pieces, the youths, the children* ...

'It is remarkably pretty; only, one remembers how it stank in that temple ...

'Those priests take out your heart as quick as a thief takes out your purse . . .'

Montezuma does not quite believe, and yet he does not quite disbelieve. Cortés has taken his mind away. There is no strength in the king. He does not pray to the earth and the wind, trying to get well.

Today Cortés accused him of Escalante's death at Vera Cruz.

He denied he had had Escalante killed.

Cortés replied, 'Then send to Vera Cruz for the chief Quapopoca who murdered Escalante and my men. Till it be decided who is guilty, come and live with me.'

Montezuma had no strength in him. Almost I prayed that he would kill Cortés and then kill himself. He only asked me whether he should go with Cortés.

I said with a shrug it would save his life maybe.

He did not go gladly, but he went.

He is really afraid that Cortés may prove to be Quetzalcoatl.

Quapopoca and his son and fifteen chiefs arrived today from the coast for judgement and justice.

Montezuma turned their case over to Cortés.

They remained silent.

Cortés decreed that they be burnt alive.

Then Quapopoca spoke and said he had only obeyed the orders of Montezuma.

Montezuma denied it. Quapopoca looked at me. I knew it was the truth.

In the courtyard the Spaniards make pyres of arrows and javelins.

The Indian princes, my brothers, die in the flames without wincing. I take my stand before their pyres and watch them die, and my heart breaks. Quapopoca gazes at me steadily, and I try to give him the strength of our Mexican earth.

Either the chiefs were guilty or Montezuma was guilty; but not both. There is no justice in Cortés, there is no justice in Montezuma.

While the chiefs burn, Cortés, to humiliate him to the utmost, puts Montezuma in gyves. With his own hands he puts gyves on the hands and feet of the great Emperor. He does not take them off till the chiefs have met the shadow. Montezuma cries like a weak woman.

These days Cortés is the serpent without feathers, the serpent of the dust, and all his ways are dusty.

It is cunning, all of it; cunning in the ways we Aztecs can be cunning, the way of the poisonous snake.

*　　　*　　　*

Tonight we are alone. I say to Cortés, 'You have destroyed fifteen beautiful human beings, who might have been your friends, and their warriors your followers. And why was it a fault in them to kill Escalante if Montezuma commanded it?'

Cortés answers: 'I will teach every Mexican to keep his hands off a Spaniard.'

I reply in turn: 'If you teach by force, then in what are you better than Montezuma and his forefathers?'

Cortés looks at me like a dog that does not understand human speech.

I have tried to prepare the bride – only for those few golden days at Cempoala did he try to prepare the groom.

I have seen the snake gliding to the pool at dusk, I have watched him sleeping in the sun, I have felt him in my own shadows, when I could not see him; yes, in my own shadows known the gliding river of his motion; and without him there is only dispossession. Should he be but venom, yet is he a real thing calling to a real thing to come to terms with it. The bite of this snake is pure: it ends the weariness of the eye to rest on figures of mercy.

Into flowers, jewels, blood, plunges the Aztec to forget. Nothing to live for but the round of sacrifice and ritual, the battlefield, the music of sad poets. To destroy the roots of life, what power equals fear? These white men are a sign from the gods, though they be not gods themselves. Montezuma is not sure. He the king fears: I the slave hope.

But I no longer feel part of these great hours, as I did at Cempoala because of love.

Montezuma and I are alone, for the first time. It is in the garden overlooking the lakes.

He loses not a minute, but says, 'Malinche, you who know this man so well, is he Quetzalcoatl?'

Montezuma grows more haggard daily.

'My Lord, though I still love Hernán Cortés so much I would even be the horse to bear him onwards, the god is not Cortés, he is *in* Cortés, hidden, undiscovered. He stirs and speaks, far away as a dream. As one might pass into a temple that is strange and not always beautiful or right, but which is the only true temple, so I pass into Cortés.

'And so I know: Quetzalcoatl has come back to us not in his own likeness. A thing has befallen Quetzalcoatl; he has been taken in the snare of his race. To free him will need love, inexhaustible love.'

'Is it true, Malinche?'

'It is true, My Lord. But it will be a long time before these newcomers are fashioned out of Mexican earth, a long time before we lose in one another our poison and our cruelty. You will be gone, and Cortés will be gone, and our grandchildren and great-grandchildren will be gone.'

Montezuma gazes at me. It is the sightless gaze of the boy I saw dismembered in the village of the dark forest.

Tonight my sisters and I talk. I turn Doña Luisa's wrist, so that the artery shows, and say: 'Look how the good blood is throbbing here. The priest can tear out a girl's heart or a boy's, but a god must put it back if it is to stay. To give heart back to body, do you think it easy? When for long ages heart has been a separate offering to palpitate sunwards?

'Our earth has borne the tread of our priests too long. Now time turns against the acrid priests – the unpredictable comes amongst us in unpredictable ways.

'There will be disguise after disguise till we see the shining limbs. The spirits who know all know what must be done, nor do they explain it to us.

'There is no choice, let the bloodshed take us.

Love is our only offering: bread, said Quetzalcoatl, the bread of life.

'I am leading the way for you. Under my heart grows the child of Cortés.'

I am helping Cortés destroy my land, and kill and torture my people.

But if I do not help him, my land will destroy Cortés.

I have had to choose. I give my life to Cortés because of the locket he bears about his throat and knows nothing about.

Later, out of his scaled armour will come Quetzalcoatl.

Later, I shall be justified. But who knows how much later?

The city in a terrible tide is rising to destroy us.

The days go by faster and faster, they blur; all the nights blur – and in this blurring Cortés recurs with demands on my pity and on my faith. His caress is fevered. We pause for a second in the shadow of death; then we go forward and are blurred again. He has just left me – he came, he went, in a whirlwind.

But I opened the locket about his neck.

'Why?' he asked me.

'I need to see again the Mother and the Child
you bring to us.'

(1 July 1520)

Montezuma is dead. The moment of his anguish
has come upon the King.

Nobody can escape the powers which made the
first world, and compose all there is in the present
world.

Tenochtitlán is no longer safe for us. The portable bridge has been prepared for the three openings
in the causeway. Cortés orders the city to be aban-
doned at midnight.

The boy Sandoval is to take the van, Cortés the
centre, Alvarado and León the rear, each with
Tlascalans.

Cortés warns the new soldiers from Vera Cruz
not to carry too much gold. He says, 'He travels
safest in the dark who travels lightest.'

Dreadful night. Cloudy, and a drizzly rain that
never stopped. Padre de la Merced said the bene-
diction. At midnight we marched down the great
street of Tlacopán, in silence and without torches.
The van reached the causeway.

The Aztec sentries at the bridge heads cried out.
No one had remembered to kill them. The priests

keeping the night watch on the summits of the pyramids understood instantly, and sounded their shells. A moment later the huge drum in the temple of the war god reverberated.

It was not long before stones and arrows began, and we heard the noise we dreaded most, paddles plashing on the lake, like a rising wind. In the darkness we saw faintly the white cotton tunics of countless warriors.

The portable bridge bore us safely over the first opening in the bridge. But then it jammed. With strength doubled by fear the soldiers tried, but they could not lift it out to carry to the second opening.

Then it became everyone for himself. The second opening filled up with the wagons of ammunition, the treasure, the bodies of soldiers whose pockets were heavy with gold. The panic spread.

Voices and trumpets: 'The devils are leaving – cut them off, kill them!' Cries of pain, death cries. The neighing of terrified horses. The smell of blood.

Left dead at the bridges were the son and the daughters of Montezuma, Cacama the lord of Tezcuco, the other hostages and prisoners, the captives, the girls of the soldiers, the daughters of the caciques, the brave soldiers of Spain and Tlascala.

Canoes came close to the bridges and took live prisoners for the sacrifices.

Dreadful night.

Nightmare in which men I did not know rendered up the flower of their life to preserve my life.

Now, this morning at Tlacopán, the sons of Xicotenga and their Tlascalans who saved us at the bridge heads deliver me and Doña Luisa to Cortés.

Pedro de Alvarado on foot, and eight men pale and bloody from wounds, come at the end of the rout.

The little train of artillery is lost. There is not a musket. All the ammunition is lost. All the treasure is lost. All Cortés's records are lost.

The young and very beautiful Doña Elvira is dead. So is Juan Velásquez de Léon, the right hand of Cortés. So is the brave Francesco de Morla.

My darling Juan de Salasar the page died beside his master.

Cortés sits beneath a great tree with his head in his hands, crying. His anguish too has come upon him.

The voice of Sandoval, of an eighteen-year-old boy grown suddenly to manhood, rings in my ears out of the dreadful night.

'We are bound to be victorious. Have trust in

God. We shall come out of this alive, and for God's good purpose.'

The valiant and spirited young Sandoval.

And under my heart the child of Cortés.

Xicotenga – Xicotenga—

This name pounds in our blood at every step of the retreat. Will the blind cacique receive us, now we are humbled in the dust? Xicotenga is our destiny. His friendship, his food and shelter, preserved us on the march up from the sea; and now in the ruins of our hopes we have only his good heart to turn to.

'And my heart knows that he will take us in,' I tell Cortés. Cortés lies beside me, shaking with chills. He tells his beads; he paces the floor.

Sometimes I think that I who am of the same substance as this earth, love Cortés the alien with a heart that is not mine.

Never have I loved him more than now when he is crushed yet fights on.

Xicotenga comes to meet us with the captains and the people. Tears stream down his face as he takes his daughter Doña Luisa in his arms; tears stream again when he embraces Mase Escasi, whose daughter Doña Elvira was lost at the bridges along with

León her husband. The Tlascalans are wailing for their dead; they are a good people, good as the red earth which gives them their maize.

'I am very grateful, Doña Marina,' says Cortés. 'Now, with Xicotenga and Mase Escasi, and the remnant of my captains, I will plan my vengeance.'

For the first time in many a night my lord is not like a man in fever who would drink, nor like one crazed with fear and confusion who snatches at a straw.

Out of the defeat Cortés lays the plans of victory. I hear the plans, he talks them in his sleep: the whole resolve and being of a man bent upon victory. The city will fall, it cannot resist such a cobweb of deathly thinking.

Cortés will destroy the city when he takes it. Then he will build it up anew.

There will be calm months. No dead men, no sacrifices.

We shall be quiet and renewed. We shall have good times and see games of some sort. And I shall bear my lord his babe.

To me, gold-coloured flowers mean timelessness, and the come and go of the streams that are eternity. I wish that Cortés might gaze at these golden flowers in the red fields and see them, now, this minute, in the fine rain. But there are things about the Mexican earth Cortés will never see, though an old man who is blind and full of days sees them perfectly. So this quiet moment it is beside Xico-tenga that I am standing, in the gateway of his placita, seeing the rain of autumn filling the golden flowers of the Tlascalan fields.

New titles in **Picador** fiction

Gravity's Rainbow £1·50
Thomas Pynchon

'If I were banished to the moon tomorrow and could take only five books along, this would be one of them' *New York Times*

'*Moby Dick* and *Ulysses* come to mind most often as one reads . . . *Gravity's Rainbow* marks an advance beyond either' *Saturday Review*

'It is a funny, disturbing, exhausting and massive novel by a remarkable mind and talent . . . it includes just about everything of importance in the loony modern world' *Time*

'A black comedy on an epic scale' *Listener*

'Prodigious, intricate, desperately funny, fiercely inventive' *Newsweek*

'Makes other novels, by comparison, a bit simple minded' *New Statesman*

'A literary equivalent of a Jumbo Jet' *Sunday Telegraph*

'The compendiousness of a Thomas Wolfe, the density of a Faulkner, the learning of a John Barth' *New Society*

A Book of Nonsense 50p
Mervyn Peake

Introduction by Maeve Gilmore

Blending fantastic imagination, poignancy and love of the ridiculous, these writings and drawings are at once magical and hilarious. As always, Mervyn Peake speaks with a voice uniquely his own.

'A genuinely haunted imagination which stamps everything he wrote or drew . . . He can try on the strangest clothes without losing his own strange identity' Norman Shrapnel, *The Guardian*

'Peake deserves a place among the eccentrics of the English tradition, alongside Sterne, Blake, Lear, Carroll and Belloc . . . how remarkably Peake foreshadowed the tragic philosopher-fool view of society that now so strongly appeals to the young' *Times Literary Supplement*

If you have any difficulty in obtaining Picador books please send purchase price plus 7p postage to PO Box 11, Falmouth, Cornwall. While every effort is made to keep prices low, it is sometimes necessary to increase them at short notice. The publishers reserve the right to show new retail prices on covers, which may differ from those previously advertised in the text or elsewhere.